Robert and the Magic String

For Jocelyn and Daniella

Robert

and the Magic String

IVAN SHERMAN

Harcourt Brace Jovanovich, Inc., New York

When Robert Hippopotamus brought home the red string, nobody was very impressed.

He showed his mother how he could write his name with the string, but Robert's mother just smiled and went on preparing dinner.

He showed his sister the string.

"When school was over," he told her, "I turned the string into a sports car and drove it all the way home."

"How wonderful!" she said. "May I have a piece of it to tie this package?"

"You don't believe me," said Robert, and he went off to tell his father about the red string.

Mr. Hippopotamus was reading his newspaper.

"Father . . ." said Robert.

"Mmmm," Mr. Hippopotamus replied.

"I found this red string at school today. I can do all kinds of things with it."

"Mmmm," said Mr. Hippopotamus as he went on reading his newspaper.

"I can write all sorts of words with the string."

"Mmmm," said Mr. Hippopotamus.

"This afternoon," Robert went on, "I put it on the floor and walked on it. Suddenly I was on a tight-rope high above the circus. There were clowns and horseback riders and everything. They were all cheering and saying that I was the bravest tight-rope walker in the whole world."

"Mmmm," said Mr. Hippopotamus as he turned the great big page of his newspaper.

Robert's pet canary loved the string. He thought it was a worm, and Robert had to pull very hard to get his red string back.

One day Robert's mother was hanging up the wash when the clothesline broke. Robert offered to let her use his string. His mother thought it would be too weak to hold so many clothes, but since there was nothing else to do, she tried it. Happily, the string held everything beautifully.

"My red string," announced Robert, "is the strongest in the world."

Mrs. Hippopotamus just smiled.

Robert would play with the string for hours. Sometimes he would make a lasso out of it. Then he could catch bulls and wild horses.

Other times he would hold tightly to one end of the string and run down the street until he rose up in the air like a kite. He would fly high above the rooftops and talk to the birds as he passed them by.

Every night at the dinner table Robert would tell his family about the wonderful things he did with his red string.

He told them how he put the red string in his mother's wash-basket. "Then sitting in front of it," he continued, "I played my flute and watched the string wriggle out of the basket like a snake."

His mother would smile as she served the broccoli and say, "How nice!"

Robert's sister would giggle behind her napkin, saying, "Such a silly child!"

Mr. Hippopotamus would look up from his lamb chops and say, "Mmmm," and reach for another portion of potatoes.

One morning while Mr. Hippopotamus was dressing to go to work, his shoelace broke.

"Now what shall I do?" he complained.

"You can use my red string," Robert offered. He helped his father lace his shoe with the string, and Mr. Hippopotamus went off to work.

Robert's father was very annoyed. Everyone at the office laughed at his red shoelace. Though Robert had wound the string around his father's ankle very carefully and tied it with a double bow, it kept opening and Mr. Hippopotamus kept tripping over it.

"I can't wait until I get home," he thought as he left the office, "so I can take off this silly string."

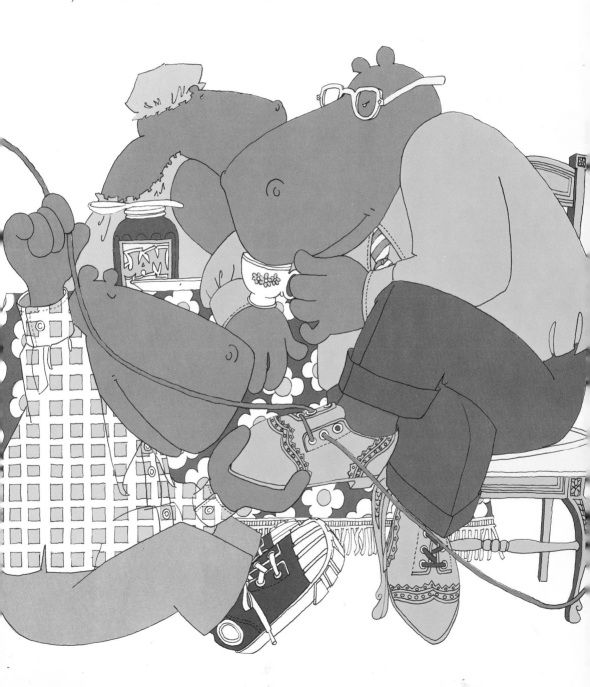

As Mr. Hippopotamus passed the bank on his way home, he noticed that the string had opened again and was trailing down the street.

As he bent over to gather up the string, he heard a shout. He looked up to see two masked men running in his direction. He tried to get out of their way, but as he turned, the men tripped over the string.

"That was clever of you," said the bank president, "tripping those bank robbers with your shoelace."

Mr. Hippopotamus smiled proudly.

"How did you come up with such a plan?" asked a television reporter who had just arrived.

"Well, just between us," Mr. Hippopotamus whispered, "I didn't do anything. I think it was this magic string that my son, Robert, found."

"Magic string?" asked the reporter, pushing his microphone at Mr. Hippopotamus. "Tell the folks at home about this magic string your son found."

"Well..." Mr. Hippopotamus was nervous now. A television camera was whirring away, and the crowd was getting bigger. "He says he can write with it."

The reporter began to giggle.

"He can turn it into a snake, and he can walk on it up in the air like a tightrope," Mr. Hippopotamus continued.

Even the people watching didn't believe Mr. Hippopotamus now.

"And he says he can fly in the air with it like a kite."

"He says he can fly?" The reporter laughed.

"Well, he can!" Mr. Hippopotamus was angry now. "I saw him do it with my own eyes."

When Mr. Hippopotamus got home, he unlaced his shoe and carefully put the string in the middle of the dining room table. Then he gathered the family around the television set and turned on the news broadcast.

When Robert's sister heard how her father captured the bank robbers, she danced around in a circle.

"Oh, Daddy," she screeched, "I'm so proud of you! I knew the minute Robert told me how he turned the string into a sports car that it was enchanted."

"All this talk about enchantment is silly," Robert's mother said. "After all, the boy was just pretending that he could do those things."

"Pretending!" said Mr. Hippopotamus in a huff. "The bank president offered me a thousand dollars for our enchanted string. He wanted to use it to tie the bank doors closed at night. Does that sound like pretending?"

They had hardly finished dinner when there was a knock at the door. In walked the first and second and third violinists of the Philharmonic Orchestra.

"What a contribution to music this string would be," the first violinist said, taking the string from the table. "If all our violins were strung with this, they would make the world's most beautiful music."

"Now that's a wonderful idea," said Mrs. Hippopotamus. "If the string can really make music," she added.

Robert was so bored that he started playing with his pet canary.

The next visitor was a five-star general.

"If we could take this string of yours apart," he said, taking the string from the violinists and putting it back on the table, "and find out what makes it work, we'd revolutionize flying. Mr. Hippopotamus," he added, "you owe it to your country."

Robert's father thought this was a splendid idea. "How famous we'd be!" he exclaimed.

"But suppose they take our string apart," Robert's sister asked, "and they don't find out what makes it work?"

Mrs. Hippopotamus began clearing the dishes from the table. Robert wandered around the room with his canary sitting atop his head.

Before they could discuss this idea further, a stranger barged in.

"There's a lot of money to be made in string," he said. "It's just a matter of knowing how."

"Money?" asked Robert's father. "We hadn't thought about money."

"It's what makes the world go," said the stranger.

Robert didn't trust this man. He stopped paying attention to his canary and watched the stranger chew on a fat cigar.

"I suppose a lot of people have been asking for that string," said the stranger, putting his fingers together and cracking his knuckles with a tremendous crunch.

"Yes," replied Mr. Hippopotamus. "We've been trying to decide who to give it to."

"Don't give it to anyone," said the visitor. "Rent it."

"Rent it?" asked Robert's father.

"Rent it?" Robert's sister asked.

"Who would want to rent a silly piece of string?" asked Mrs. Hippopotamus.

The stranger grinned broadly and rubbed his hands together.

"When a king has his appendix removed," the stranger began, "he doesn't want to be stitched with common thread! And the son of a billionaire," the stranger continued, "shouldn't play cat's cradle with ordinary string—not when he can rent our magic string."

Everyone sat spellbound, staring at the man. No one even noticed Robert's pet canary pecking at the bread crumbs on the dining room table.

"There are Yo-yo champions who'd give anything to rent our magic string. I could go on and on, but first let me see this wondrous string of ours."

"It's right there on the dining room table," said Mr. Hippopotamus. They all turned to the table just in time to see Robert's pet canary swallow the last bit of the enchanted red string.

The very next day Robert found the most marvelous broom-stick. If he sat on it, he could ride it like a horse. If he swung it, he could hit a baseball a jillion miles, and if he held it like a rifle, he could hunt lions and tigers.

But he never told anyone about it.